MULTIVERSE TRAVELLERS

MULTIVERSE TRAVELLERS

Pragati Mukherjee

EXCELLER BOOKS®
A GLOBAL PRESS

Multiverse Travellers

Cover by Exceller Books using resources from Pixabay.com

ISBN: 978-93-48892-43-0

Published in India in 2025 by Exceller Books,
An imprint of GE Group,
G1, Dream Apartment, Degree College Road, Belgharia,
Kolkata, 700056, India
www.excellerbooks.com

EXCELLER BOOKS®
A GLOBAL PRESS

Dedication

This book is dedicated to the dreamers and the real-life explorers alike. This book is also dedicated to real "universe travellers", mentioned as the scientists and astronauts at NASA, USA. They might not be going to other universes (because we don't even know if those exist!), but they do something just as amazing. They go into space and explore our own huge universe, studying planets and stars. It's like they're discovering new places within our own reality.

So, if you like non-fictional, realistic, factual stories about exploring new worlds, or if you're amazed by what scientists and astronauts are doing to learn about our universe, then this book is dedicated to you. It's dedicated to the dreamers and the real-life explorers alike.

ACKNOWLEDGMENT

A heartfelt thank you extends to my incredible parents, Jhiimli Mukherjee and Dr. Pratap Mukherjee—the very individuals who have nurtured my imagination and fostered a deep appreciation for the boundless knowledge of this non-fictional, realistic, factual wonders book, which is further explored by the brilliant minds at the NASA Space Centre in the USA. While this novel, *Multiverse Travellers*, ventures into the non-realistic territory of inter-dimensional journeys, the underlying spirit of exploration and the human drive to uncover the unknown are reflections of the very real dedication exemplified by scientists like those at NASA. Your unwavering support and encouragement have been the bedrock upon which this creative endeavour was built.

To my mother, Jhiimli Mukherjee—your artistic soul and storytelling prowess have been a constant source of inspiration. Your ability to weave narratives and spark the imagination has undoubtedly influenced the fantastical elements within these pages. Thank you for nurturing the dreamer in me and for always believing in the power of stories to transport us to new and exciting worlds, even if those worlds exist only within the realm of fiction.

To my father, Dr. Pratap Mukherjee—your distinguished career as a doctor has always motivated and emboldened me to take up challenging tasks and will continue to do so in the years to come.

This novel, *Multiverse Travellers*, is a testament to the human fascination with the unknown—a fascination that is equally present in the fictional leaps of inter-dimensional travel and the factual advancements made by NASA in exploring our own universe. It is with immense gratitude and love that I dedicate this work to you both, Jhiimli Mukherjee and Dr. Pratap Mukherjee—my guiding stars and the true explorers of my own world. Thank you for everything.

TABLE OF CONTENTS

The Trouble

The New World

The Future

The Beginning

An Invitation to Wonder

The idea of *Multiverse Travellers*—people leaping between universes, meeting other versions of themselves, or exploring realities stranger than imagination—belongs, for now, to the realm of story. NASA scientists don't step through portals into other dimensions. They don't encounter alien festivals or sign treaties with beings from beyond the stars.

And yet, the spirit of exploration that drives these tales is very real. Every time a scientist launches a telescope, studies a distant galaxy, or sends a spacecraft into the unknown, they are, in a sense, our own "multiverse travellers." They push the boundaries of what we know, searching for surprises hidden in the fabric of reality.

This book is not a scientific manual, nor is it meant to predict the future. Instead, it is a collection of speculative snapshots—short chapters that ask *what if?* What if someone from another universe appeared tomorrow with warnings? What if art, music, and sport were

shared across countless worlds? What if love itself could transcend the boundaries of reality?
These are not predictions; they are possibilities. They are invitations to imagine, to question, and to dream. Just as scientists study the universe to uncover truth, these stories explore the multiverse to uncover wonder.

I invite you to read these chapters as thought experiments—little journeys into ideas that could reshape how we see our own universe. Because while the multiverse may remain beyond our reach, curiosity, discovery, and imagination are within us all.

THE BEGINNING

1

The Strange Event

Something unexpected happens, breaking the rules of our world.

The Strange Event is about when a scientist – Dr. Aris Throne – sees something surprising that doesn't fit with what we already know about the universe. This unexpected thing is what makes us start looking into new ideas. Imagine NASA scientist Dr. Aris Throne discovering something unusual in space—maybe a star behaving in a way we didn't think it could, or a planet that looks completely different from anything seen before. These surprising things, the ones that don't match our current understanding, are like the "strange event" that makes scientists ask new questions and try to figure out what's going on.

When scientists encounter something strange like this, it doesn't just end there. It actually opens new paths for science. Even though we do not yet have proof of other universes, if a scientist—like

Dr. Aris Throne—ever found something that hinted at them, that would be a very strange event and would spark an entirely new way of thinking. In the same way, when NASA makes a big, surprising discovery—such as finding a new kind of energy in space or seeing galaxies connected in an unexpected way—it inspires new studies and ideas to explain what's been observed.

Even though NASA isn't sending people to other universes, the work they do constantly reveals new and sometimes strange things in our own. Every time they launch a new telescope or study fresh data, they may see something that changes how we think about space. These discoveries are not like opening doors to other worlds, but they are vital for science. They make us rethink old ideas and come up with new ways to understand the amazing universe we live in. NASA's work is all about finding these strange events—and learning from them.

2

The First Look

A scientist notices this strange event and wonders if there are other worlds.

Dr. Aris Thorne, a NASA scientist, leaned over streams of data flowing in from the James Webb Telescope. Among the numbers and signals, something unusual caught his eye—a faint but repeating pulse of energy, unlike anything they had seen before. It wasn't random noise. It wasn't a glitch in the machinery. It was steady, deliberate, and strange.

He ran the checks. Again and again, he tested for errors. Was it interference from Earth? A calibration issue? Cosmic background radiation? Each possibility fell away. The signal remained, quiet but insistent, as though it had been waiting to be noticed.

At first, Thorne resisted letting his imagination run ahead of the evidence. Science demands patience, and he was cautious not to let speculation outpace fact. But the longer he stared at the data, the more unsettling a thought began to stir: could this energy be a sign of something beyond their universe? Other worlds, other realities—theories with no proof, but now impossible to ignore.

The signal was not just a curiosity; it was an invitation to rethink. Thorne knew discoveries often begin this way—with anomalies, with things that don't fit neatly into the models. And sometimes, those anomalies open entire new paths for science.

Late into the night, he drafted a preliminary report. The signal, he wrote, was unusual, persistent, and unexplained. Its origin was unknown, and further investigation would be required. Perhaps it came from some hidden corner of space. Or perhaps—he hesitated even to put the words on paper—it came from somewhere else entirely.

3

The Idea

A scientist suggests that there may be many other universes

After days of staring at the repeating signal, Dr. Aris Thorne found his thoughts drifting toward possibilities he had never dared to take seriously. What if the universe we knew—the galaxies, stars, planets, and all the laws of physics—was only one of many?

He recalled theories whispered on the edges of cosmology, models that suggested countless other universes could exist, each with their own histories, their own rules of reality. Some might resemble ours. Others might be unrecognizably strange.

The signal refused to fit within the patterns of known science. It was not noise, not an error, not anything familiar. And so Thorne let his imagination, anchored by science, take one cautious step further. What if this strange pulse was not from within our universe at all? What if it was a fragment of something beyond—an echo, or perhaps even a whisper, from another world entirely?

It was not proof. It was not even a hypothesis yet. But for Thorne, the idea was enough to shift the ground beneath his feet. For the first time, the possibility of many universes no longer belonged only to equations and thought experiments. It might be waiting, out there, sending signals across the dark.

4

The Doubters

Most people do not believe this scientist

When Dr. Thorne carefully shared his strange signal and the idea of different universes with other scientists, most of them didn't believe him. They were used to the way things are and had seen no real proof of other universes. To them, his ideas sounded unlikely, and they assumed there must be a standard explanation for the signal—even if it hadn't been found yet.

This moment shows the challenge new ideas face in science. No matter how exciting a possibility may be, excellent proof is required to change what everyone already believes. It becomes a struggle between bold imagination and the cautious, evidence-first approach that science demands.

5

The Big Discovery

A lucky accident helps them build a machine that allows them to travel between worlds

Years pass after the strange signal, and while most scientists remain unconvinced about other universes, Dr. Aris Thorne and a small group of colleagues refuse to let the mystery fade. They continue to study the data, running experiments in hopes of finding a clue that could explain what they once saw.

Then, something unexpected happens. During an unrelated experiment with tiny particles meant to probe the nature of the signal, a sudden burst of energy appears. For a brief moment, space itself seems to bend, and a small opening—like a doorway—flickers into view. Through it, they glimpse what looks like another world. The hole vanishes almost as quickly as it appeared, but the moment is undeniable.

It is a lucky accident, yet one with profound meaning. The team realises that if such an opening can happen once, it might be possible to create it again—deliberately. Perhaps even build a machine that could allow travel between worlds.

This discovery, born not from certainty but from chance, changes everything. Sometimes the universe reveals its secrets not when we are searching hardest, but when we stumble unexpectedly into the unknown.

6

The First Trip

Someone bravely tries travelling to another world for the first time

After the accidental opening, Dr. Thorne's team works in secrecy for years, refining their experiments and slowly constructing a machine capable of opening doorways to other worlds. The work is painstaking, uncertain, and often doubted even by the scientists themselves. Yet, piece by piece, the impossible begins to take shape.

At last, the machine stands ready for its first true test. The room is filled with a tense, electric silence. The team knows what's at stake—this is more than an experiment; it is a step into the unknown.

Dr. Lena Hanson, a brilliant and fearless member of the group, volunteers to be the first. She has studied every calculation, every risk, and every precaution, and she knows the dangers better than anyone. Still, she steps forward, steady and determined. For the first time in human history, someone prepares to cross into another world.

7

The Mystery

The traveller comes back changed, unable to explain what happened

Dr. Lena Hanson returns from her trip. Physically, she is unharmed, but something about her has changed. Her eyes seem distant, her voice slower, as though part of her is still elsewhere.

When the team asks what she saw, she struggles to find words. Her memories slip away like fragments of a dream. She recalls flashes of light, shifting shapes, and feelings she cannot explain, but nothing clear, nothing solid. Was it a place? Were there people? She cannot say.

The scientists record everything, yet the mystery only deepens. The journey proves that travel between worlds is possible, but it leaves them with more questions than answers. What are these universes really like? And why can't Lena describe what she experienced?

8

The Fear

People worry about the dangers of travelling to other worlds.

When rumours spread about the possibility of travelling to other worlds, fear begins to take hold. People worry about what dangers might be waiting beyond the doorway—unknown landscapes, hostile beings, or forces that could harm their own world if brought back.

Governments, too, grow uneasy. Their concern is not only about safety but also about power. Who would control this technology? Could one nation use it to gain an advantage over others? The discovery that once promised wonder now begins to stir suspicion and caution.

Fear of the unknown, it seems, rises just as quickly as curiosity. Every great leap in science brings both excitement and unease, and the question of other worlds is no different.

9

The Secret Work

The government secretly continues to study travel between worlds

The scientists know that travelling to other worlds carries both great promise and great danger. Soon, governments step in, quietly taking control of the research. What began as open curiosity now moves into hidden laboratories and classified projects.

Dr. Thorne's team, who only wanted to understand the universe, suddenly find themselves bound by secrecy. They are no longer free explorers but researchers working under strict orders. The government's questions are different from theirs—less about discovery, more about control. Could this technology be used for power, for advantage, for purposes far from pure science?

What was once a search for knowledge now lives in the shadows, where motives shift and the truth becomes harder to see.

10

The Hidden Lab

They built a special, secret place to work on this technology

To guard the secret of inter-dimensional travel, the government builds a hidden laboratory, tucked far from public sight. No maps mark its location. No outsider knows its name. Inside, walls hum with advanced machines, and only a handful of carefully chosen scientists and engineers are allowed to enter.

Here, in silence and secrecy, they press forward with their experiments—trying to open and control the strange doorways to other worlds. Every test brings both wonder and unease. Behind the locked doors of the hidden lab, the question grows larger: are they uncovering knowledge... or inviting dangers no one can predict?

THE EXPLORERS

11

The Chosen Ones

A special team is picked to explore other worlds

The strange energy signal that Dr. Aris Thorne first detected at NASA never faded. Years of relentless study had turned it into something more—small, flickering doorways to other realities, like fleeting cracks in the wall of our universe. Each glimpse suggested possibilities too vast to ignore, and too dangerous to leave to chance.

From these shadows of discovery, a team was chosen. Not only scientists, but explorers of many kinds—linguists, biologists, survival experts—each selected with the same care once given to astronauts. They would need to decipher unknown languages, study life that might not follow Earth's rules, and survive in worlds where nothing could be assumed.

They were brave, quick-thinking, and adaptable. They became the first "multiverse explorers," venturing into realities that Dr. Thorne's initial discovery hinted at. Just like early explorers on Earth needed special skills to navigate new lands, this team needed to be prepared for anything these other universes might hold. They were the chosen ones to take the first big step into the unknown, based on Dr. Thorne's ground-breaking work.

12

The Training

The team trains hard for the dangers of travel.

Knowing that travelling to other universes could be very risky, the chosen team went through serious training. They practised for all sorts of weird things they might find – different air, strange gravity, and even meeting creatures they'd never seen before. It was like NASA's astronaut training, but pushed further into speculation, because no one could say for certain what awaited them in the realities hinted at by Dr. Thorne's signal.

They studied how to protect themselves from unknown microbes, how to attempt communication with non-human intelligences, and how to keep calm in landscapes that might defy logic or feel disturbingly unreal. This training showed how important it was to be prepared for anything when exploring the multiverse, a journey made possible by Dr. Thorne's initial strange discovery. The team had to be tough and smart to face the challenges that lay ahead.

13

The First Journey

The team travels to another Earth

The day finally arrived. Years of hidden work, cautious experiments, and relentless doubt had led to this moment. The machine, born from Dr. Thorne's first strange signal, hummed with a deep resonance, opening a doorway that shimmered like liquid light. Instruments suggested what lay beyond was not some alien void but another version of Earth—an echo of their own world, repeating across the fabric of universes.

Crossing through was disorienting. The team felt their bodies lurch, as if pulled sideways through reality itself, before the dizziness cleared and they stood on solid ground. At first glance it was Earth—blue skies, air they could breathe, landscapes that carried a sense of home. And yet, something was off. The shadows were a fraction too sharp, the light just a little strange, as though reality here obeyed rules bent ever so slightly from their own.

It was a moment of breathtaking confirmation. Dr. Thorne's unsettling thought—that his signal hinted at other universes—was no longer theory. The team's first steps on this other Earth proved that the boundaries of reality were more porous than anyone had dared imagine. Excitement and unease tangled in their chests as they looked out over the new world, fully aware that nothing about science—or existence—would ever be the same again.

14

The Mirror World

They find a world very similar to ours, but with small differences.

As the team explored this other Earth – a world made accessible by the technology stemming from Dr. Aris Thorne's research – they were struck by how much it resembled home. There were continents, oceans, and even plants and animals that seemed familiar.

But the deeper they looked, the more the strangeness revealed itself. A city skyline shimmered in the distance, yet its towers spiralled in unfamiliar patterns. Plants bore unearthly colors. It was as if evolution had slipped, just slightly, and found another route – like history had taken a slightly different turn, or technology had developed in a new way. It was like seeing our own world in a mirror, but the reflection had some surprising changes, showing that even universes that seem alike can have their own unique stories – something Dr. Aris Thorne had only theorised about.

15

The Surprise

They meet creatures they've never seen before in this new world.

While exploring a forest that seemed similar to ones on their own Earth – a forest in this world reached because of Dr. Thorne's invention – the team had a huge surprise. They came across living things that were completely new to them. These weren't just slightly different animals; they were creatures that had evolved in entirely different ways in this other universe. It was a discovery far beyond what Dr. Thorne's initial signal could have predicted.

This encounter showed the incredible variety of life that might exist across the multiverse. These creatures, unlike anything on their home world, highlighted the potential for completely alien biology – something that Dr. Thorne's team had only speculated about based on the faint signals they had detected. It was a moment that truly emphasised the "new" in this new world.

16

The First Meeting

The world-travel machine begins to fail, threatening their fragile first contact.

When the team encountered these new creatures – life forms made accessible by the travel technology born from Dr. Thorne's research – they knew they had to try and communicate. The scientists who specialised in language and communication carefully tried to find a way to talk to them.

They used pictures, simple maths ideas, and tried to use gestures that might be universal. It was a difficult and tense situation because they had no idea how these creatures thought or what kind of language they might use. This first attempt at talking was a big step in understanding this new world and its inhabitants – a challenge made possible by Dr. Thorne's initial foray into the unknown.

The team had to be patient and observant, trying to find any common ground with these completely new beings. It was a real test of their

skills and their hopes for peaceful interaction in these other realities that Dr. Thorne's work had opened up.

17

The Culture Shock

A special team is picked to explore other worlds.

The strange energy signal first detected by Dr. Aris Thorne at NASA didn't just fade away. After years of intense research, Thorne and his team managed to create small, unstable doorways to what appeared to be other realities, much like fleeting glimpses through a crack in a wall. Recognizing the immense potential and inherent dangers, a special team was assembled.

The Culture Shock: The team is surprised by how different life is in this new world.

As the team spent more time on this other Earth, a world they could reach because of the technology Dr. Thorne helped create, they started to see that even though it looked similar to home, the way the intelligent beings lived was very different. Their societies, their customs, what they thought was important – it was all surprising and new. It was like visiting a foreign country on Earth, but even more different, showing how varied life and society could be across the multiverse, a concept Dr. Thorne's initial discovery had hinted at.

The team had to learn quickly and try to understand these new ways of life, even when they were confusing or unexpected. This experience showed them that exploring other universes wasn't just about seeing new places and creatures, but also about understanding completely different ways of living and thinking, a journey that began with Dr. Thorne's first look at that strange signal.

18

The Unwanted Changes

The team's actions in this new world cause problems they didn't expect.

When the team went to that other Earth – the one they could reach because of Dr. Aris Thorne's discovery – things didn't go exactly as planned. Maybe when they tried to talk to the strange creatures, it scared them or made them angry. Or maybe just by being there, the team brought tiny bugs or messed up the nature of that other world in ways they didn't mean to. This showed them that even if you have good intentions, going to other universes (like Dr. Thorne first found a hint of) can be risky and cause problems you didn't see coming.

These unexpected problems made things tough for the team. They went there to explore and learn, like NASA scientists study new planets, but what they did had bad side effects. It made them think hard about whether it was right to even go to other worlds in the first place, something that

Dr. Thorne's work had made possible. The team now had to deal with the trouble they caused in a world that wasn't theirs, and that was much harder than just looking around.

19

The Return Home

The team comes back to their own world, changed by their adventure.

After dealing with the unexpected trouble on that other Earth – trouble that happened because they could travel there thanks to Dr. Aris Thorne's work – the team finally came back to their own universe. Going back through the doorway between worlds, a technology that started with Thorne's strange signal, made them tired and emotional. Seeing other realities and meeting alien creatures really changed them.

Just like astronauts who go to space see Earth in a new way when they return, these multiverse explorers were different after their trip. They had learned so much and seen things that changed how they thought about their own world. Their journey, which began with Dr. Thorne's curious discovery, had changed them forever.

20

The Ripple Effect

The things they did in the other world start to affect their own world.

Coming back home – to the world Dr. Aris Thorne first studied – didn't end their connection to that other Earth. Things they had done there started to have effects back in their own universe. Maybe they accidentally brought back some tiny living thing that started to spread, or maybe a piece of technology from the other world caused problems with their own technology.

This "ripple effect" showed that the different universes might be connected in ways they didn't fully understand, something that Dr. Thorne's early theories might have touched on. The team and the scientists back home, who were once excited about traveling to other worlds, now had to face the serious dangers of messing with other realities. It was a big warning about how careful they needed to be when exploring the multiverse, a possibility that all started with Dr. Thorne's strange observation.

THE TROUBLE

21

The Machine Problems

The machine for traveling between worlds starts to break.

The machine that allowed travel between universes—the one built based on Dr. Thorne's initial research—started to have problems. It wasn't working as smoothly as it used to. Sometimes the doorways to other worlds would flicker and close unexpectedly, or the machine would make strange noises and give off unusual readings. It was clear that pushing the boundaries of reality was taking a toll on the technology that made it possible.

The team of scientists and engineers worked hard to try to fix the machine, but the problems seemed to be getting worse. They didn't fully understand the stresses that inter-dimensional travel was putting on their creation. It was like trying to use a tool for something it was never really meant to do, and now it was starting to fall apart under the strain of bending the laws of physics.

These machine problems were a major setback for the exploration of the multiverse. Not only did they make traveling to other worlds more dangerous and unpredictable, but they also raised questions about the long-term viability of this technology. The very thing that had opened up the possibility of exploring other realities was now threatening to close those doors forever.

Dr. Thorne and his team realised that they were dealing with forces they didn't fully comprehend. The breakdown of the machine was a stark reminder that their understanding of the multiverse and how to interact with it was still very limited. They needed to figure out what was causing the machine to fail—not just to continue exploring, but perhaps to prevent even bigger problems down the line.

22

The Secret Travellers

People who shouldn't be travelling to other worlds.

As the inter-dimensional travel technology became more developed (though still facing problems), it wasn't just the carefully chosen exploration team using it. Word started to get out, and some individuals and groups who weren't supposed to know about it found ways to access the machine or build their own crude versions. These "secret travellers" had their own reasons for wanting to go to other worlds, and their actions were often reckless and unplanned.

These unauthorised trips created even more chaos and potential danger. These secret travellers were not trained or prepared for the realities of other universes. They might have been going for personal gain, to steal technology, or simply out of curiosity—without understanding the potential consequences of their actions on both our world and the worlds they were visiting.

The team and the authorities struggled to control this unauthorised travel. It was like trying to keep a powerful secret when the genie was already starting to get out of the bottle. These secret travellers added another layer of complexity to an already delicate situation, increasing the risk of unwanted interactions and further destabilising the fragile connections between worlds that Dr. Thorne's work had revealed.

The actions of these secret travellers made it clear that the ability to travel between universes was a powerful and dangerous tool that needed to be carefully controlled. Their selfish or misguided journeys threatened to undo any good that might come from responsible exploration and raised the stakes of the entire inter-dimensional endeavour.

23

The Attacks

People from other worlds start to come to our world and cause trouble.

The opening of pathways between worlds, initially a scientific breakthrough based on Dr. Thorne's research, began to have a dark side. It wasn't just people from our world going to others; beings from other universes started coming to our world, and they weren't always friendly. These visitors often had their own agendas, which sometimes involved causing trouble, taking resources, or even trying to exert power over our reality.

These attacks created fear and confusion. People on our Earth didn't understand who these invaders were or why they were coming. It was a terrifying realisation that the multiverse wasn't just a place to explore; it could also be a source of danger. The safety and security of their own world were now being threatened by forces from beyond their known reality.

The exploration team and the authorities had to quickly learn how to defend themselves against these inter-dimensional threats. They had to study the technology and abilities of these invaders and try to understand their motives. The focus shifted from peaceful exploration to urgent defence, as the consequences of opening these pathways became increasingly violent.

Dr. Aris Thorne and his colleagues felt a heavy responsibility, as their initial discoveries had inadvertently led to this crisis. They now had to use their knowledge of the multiverse to find ways to protect their world from these unwanted visitors, turning their scientific pursuit into a desperate fight for survival.

24

The Big Crisis

The machine breaks badly, causing chaos across many worlds.

The already unstable inter-dimensional travel machine finally broke down in a catastrophic way. This wasn't just a simple malfunction; it was a major failure that had far-reaching consequences across multiple universes, all linked by the pathways that Dr. Thorne's work had initially opened. The breakdown caused energy surges, tears in the fabric of reality, and unpredictable shifts between worlds.

The chaos was immense. People and objects were being randomly pulled between universes, causing confusion and panic on multiple Earths and potentially other realities as well. The delicate balance between worlds was shattered, and the very structure of the multiverse seemed to be at risk of collapsing. The technology that was meant for exploration had become a source of widespread disaster.

The team realised the gravity of the situation. The machine wasn't just a tool; it was a nexus point, and its destruction was having a domino effect across realities. The potential for widespread destruction and the unravelling of the multiverse became terrifyingly real. The dream of peaceful exploration had turned into a nightmare of inter-dimensional catastrophe.

Dr. Thorne and the remaining scientists knew they had to act fast. The machine's breakdown was a direct threat to their own world and countless others. They had to find a way to stabilise the inter-dimensional connections and repair the machine before the chaos consumed everything.

25

The Race Against Time

The team must fix the machine before everything falls apart.

With the inter-dimensional machine critically damaged and chaos spreading across multiple realities (a crisis directly linked to Dr. Thorne's initial breakthroughs), the remaining team found themselves in a desperate race against time. They had to understand the cause of the catastrophic failure and find a way to repair the machine before the damage became irreversible and the connections between worlds completely collapsed.

Working under immense pressure, the scientists and engineers pored over schematics, analysed energy readings, and tried to piece together the sequence of events that led to the breakdown. They faced the daunting task of fixing a technology that pushed the very limits of their understanding of the universe, all while the consequences of its failure were unfolding around them.

The team had to overcome not only the technical challenges of repairing the machine but also the logistical nightmare of dealing with the inter-dimensional chaos. They needed to find a way to stabilise the rifts between worlds and prevent further unpredictable shifts while simultaneously working on the core problem. The fate of multiple realities rested on their ability to succeed against impossible odds.

Driven by a sense of responsibility for the crisis that their exploration had inadvertently triggered, the team pushed themselves to their limits. Sleep became a luxury, and every moment was spent trying to find a solution. The initial excitement of discovery had been replaced by a desperate urgency to save not just their own world, but the entire interconnected multiverse.

26

The Sacrifices

The team might have to do something very difficult to save everyone.

As the crisis caused by the broken inter-dimensional machine worsened, the team began to realise that fixing it might not be enough. They might have to make incredibly difficult choices, potentially involving great personal sacrifice, to save their own world and the other realities that were now in danger because of the pathways Dr. Thorne's work had opened.

These potential sacrifices weighed heavily on the team. They had started as explorers, driven by curiosity, but now they faced the possibility of having to give up something precious – perhaps their own lives, their relationships, or even the future they had envisioned – to prevent the collapse of the multiverse. The weight of this responsibility was immense.

The difficult decisions they faced highlighted the profound ethical dilemmas that came with the power to travel between worlds. The initial excitement of discovery had led to a situation where saving countless lives might require individual loss. The team had to confront the true cost of their ambition and the potential consequences of tampering with the fundamental structure of reality.

It would emphasise the courage and selflessness required to face such impossible choices in the face of a universal crisis, a crisis born from the very act of exploration that Dr. Thorne had initiated.

27

The Hidden Enemy

A powerful and dangerous being is secretly causing all these problems.

As the team struggled to fix the broken inter-dimensional machine and deal with the chaos spreading across the multiverse (a chaos that followed Dr. Thorne's initial discoveries), they began to suspect that the problems weren't just accidents. There were subtle clues and inconsistencies that suggested a more sinister force at play, a hidden hand deliberately causing the strange events, the machine malfunctions, and the attacks from other worlds.

This realisation shifted the focus from simply fixing a machine to uncovering a potential enemy, a powerful being with a motive for destabilising the multiverse. This enemy had been working in the shadows, manipulating events to their own advantage, and the team's initial exploration had unknowingly played into their plans. The crisis wasn't just a technological failure; it was potentially a deliberate act of sabotage.

The team had to use all their intelligence and resources to try and identify this hidden enemy. They analysed the strange events, looked for patterns in the machine's failures, and tried to understand who might benefit from the chaos. The stakes were raised even higher, as they now faced not just a mechanical problem but a sentient and malevolent force.

Dr. Thorne, reflecting on his initial discoveries, might have realised that the strange energy signals he first detected weren't just natural phenomena but perhaps a form of communication or a byproduct of this hidden enemy's activities. The exploration that began with scientific curiosity had now become a hunt for a dangerous and unseen adversary.

28

The Big Secret

The team learns a shocking truth about these other worlds.

In their desperate attempt to understand the crisis and potentially the hidden enemy, the team uncovers a shocking truth about the other worlds they had accessed through the technology derived from Dr. Thorne's research. This secret goes beyond simple differences in history or biology; it's something fundamental about the nature of these realities or their connection to their own universe that they never could have imagined.

This big secret could be anything from the true origin of the multiverse to the real purpose behind the strange energy signals Dr. Thorne initially detected. It might reveal a hidden history, a dangerous prophecy, or a fundamental law of reality that had been previously unknown. This revelation changes everything they thought they understood about the multiverse and their place within it.

The discovery of this secret has a profound impact on the team's mission. It might change their goals, their strategies, and even their allegiances. The simple act of exploration has led them to uncover a truth that could have unimaginable consequences for all the worlds connected by their machine.

Dr. Thorne, reflecting on his initial pursuit of knowledge, might realise that the universe held secrets far greater and more dangerous than he ever anticipated. The big secret forces the team to confront the true significance of their actions and the potential ramifications of their intrusion into the complexities of the multiverse travellers.

29

The Turning Point

The team must fight this dangerous being to save all the worlds.

With the identity of the hidden enemy revealed and the shocking truth about the multiverse now known, the team reaches a turning point. They realise that simply fixing the machine isn't enough; they must directly confront the powerful and dangerous being who has been manipulating events and threatening the stability of all realities connected by the technology that Dr. Thorne's work enabled.

This confrontation marks a shift from exploration and scientific problem solving to a direct conflict. The team must now use all their knowledge, skills, and courage to stand against a foe whose power and motivations are likely far beyond anything they have encountered before. The fate of multiple universes hangs in the balance.
The battle against this hidden enemy will likely require the team to make difficult choices and

potentially use the inter-dimensional travel technology in ways they never intended. They might have to forge alliances with beings from other worlds or find unexpected strengths within themselves to face this ultimate threat.

Dr. Thorne's initial pursuit of knowledge has led to this critical juncture. The team, inspired by his initial curiosity and driven by the need to rectify the crisis that their explorations uncovered, must now become warriors to protect the delicate balance of the multiverse and secure the future of all realities.

THE NEW WORLD

30

The Aftermath

The world is changed forever by the crisis.

After the big trouble with the broken machine and the fight against the dangerous being (all because Dr. Thorne first found those strange signals), the world was never the same again. Things didn't just go back to normal. People knew that other universes were real, and that changed how they thought about everything. The idea that our world was the only one was gone forever, replaced by the knowledge of countless other realities out there.

Our own world had been through a lot. There were places that had been damaged by things coming over from other universes, and there were new technologies that had been learned from those other worlds—some good and some maybe not so good. The way people lived, the things they believed, and even the way countries worked together had all been shaken up by the crisis and the knowledge of the multiverse that Dr. Thorne's work had unveiled.

The way science was done also changed completely. Now, it wasn't just about exploring our own universe; scientists had to study the multiverse, figure out its rules, and understand the connections between all the different realities. Dr. Thorne's initial small team had grown into a huge international effort, trying to learn everything they could about the vastness beyond their own world. It was a brand-new field of study, born from a crisis but full of possibilities.

Even though the danger had passed, there was still a sense of caution and wonder about the multiverse. People knew that traveling to other worlds had risks, but they were also curious about what else was out there. The idea of new resources, new knowledge, and even new forms of life in other universes was exciting, but the memory of the crisis kept everyone aware of the potential dangers that came with such power.

The world after the crisis was a "new world" in many ways. It was a world that knew it was just one of many, a world that had been changed by the adventure and the danger of exploring the multiverse that Dr. Thorne's initial discoveries had opened up. It was a world facing a future full of both incredible possibilities and serious responsibilities as humanity learned to live in a much larger, more complex reality than they had ever imagined.

31

The New Rules

New rules are made to control travel between worlds.

After all the chaos and danger caused by uncontrolled travel between universes (a problem that arose after Dr. Thorne's initial breakthrough), everyone realised that things couldn't just go on as they were. There was a clear need for rules—new rules to decide who could go to other worlds, how they could go, and what they could do there. It was like realising that a new, powerful technology needed to be managed carefully to prevent more trouble.

The NASA scientists, governments from all over the world, and even people who had travelled to other universes came together to try and figure out these new rules. They had learned the hard way that the multiverse wasn't just a place for fun or easy exploration; it was complex and potentially dangerous. They needed to think about safety, about not hurting other universes, and about making sure that travel between worlds was done responsibly.

One of the first new rules was about who could travel. It wasn't just anyone anymore. Special teams, carefully chosen and highly trained (building on the lessons learned from the first explorers), were the only ones allowed to go. They had to follow strict guidelines and have clear reasons for their journeys—usually for scientific research or to help fix problems that had been caused earlier.

Another important rule was about what you could and couldn't take to other worlds, and what you could bring back. They didn't want to accidentally spread diseases or introduce dangerous technologies. There were also rules about interacting with the people or creatures in other universes, emphasising observation and respect rather than interference. It was all about trying to be good neighbours in the vast multiverse that Dr. Thorne's work had revealed.

To make sure the new rules were followed, a special international organisation was created. This group had the job of overseeing all travel between worlds, approving missions, and making sure everyone was acting responsibly. It was like a global space agency, but for the entire multiverse. They had to balance the desire for exploration with the need to protect all the different realities.

The new rules marked a shift in how humanity viewed the multiverse. It wasn't just a place to visit anymore; it was a complex web of interconnected realities that needed to be approached with caution, respect, and a strong sense of responsibility. The lessons learned from the crisis, which began with Dr. Thorne's initial, innocent discovery, had led to a new era of carefully managed inter-dimensional interaction, focused on understanding and preserving the delicate balance of the "new world" of the multiverse.

32

The World Ambassadors

The team becomes guides and helpers for travel between worlds.

After the new rules for travelling between worlds were put in place, the original team of explorers, who had learned so much from their first journeys (all thanks to the pathways opened by Dr. Thorne's work), took on a new role. They became like "World Ambassadors," using their experience to guide and help others who were now permitted to travel to different universes. They were the ones who had seen it all firsthand and understood the wonders and the dangers of the multiverse.

Having already made those first brave steps into the unknown, the team had a unique understanding of what to expect in other realities. They knew about the different environments, the potential challenges in communicating with alien beings, and the subtle but important differences between seemingly similar worlds. This knowledge made them invaluable as guides for new travellers.

Being in the job as World Ambassadors involved helping scientists from different fields conduct research in other universes safely and responsibly. They would lead biologists to study alien ecosystems, assist linguists in trying to understand new forms of communication, and guide geologists in examining the unique landscapes of other worlds. They were the bridge between our world's curiosity and the realities of the multiverse.

Beyond just guiding scientists, the team also played a crucial role in helping to build understanding and even peaceful relationships between different universes. If people from another world needed help or wanted to learn about our world, the Ambassadors were often the first point of contact, using their experience to foster positive interactions and prevent misunderstandings.

They undertook the important task of teaching new travellers about the rules and the reasons behind them. They emphasised the need for respect for other cultures and environments, stressing the lessons learned from the earlier crisis about the potential for unintended harm. They were the keepers of the wisdom gained from the initial, sometimes difficult, explorations made possible by Dr. Thorne's pioneering work.

In a way, the team became symbols of this new era of carefully managed multiverse interaction. They represented the transition from reckless exploration to responsible stewardship. Their journey from being the first to step into the unknown to becoming the guides for others showed how much had been learned and how the understanding of the multiverse had matured since Dr. Thorne's initial, groundbreaking discovery.

In this "New World" shaped by the opening of pathways to other universes, the original team of multiverse travellers became the World Ambassadors. They used their hard-earned experience to help others explore safely, build bridges between worlds, and ensure that the vast potential of the multiverse was approached with wisdom and a deep sense of responsibility, honouring the legacy of Dr. Thorne's initial steps into the unknown.

33

The Age of Exploration

People start exploring many different worlds.

A new era began – "The Age of Exploration" of the multiverse travellers. It wasn't a wild, uncontrolled rush like before the crisis, but a more organised and careful expansion into the many different realities that Dr. Aris Thorne's initial work had revealed. People from our world, following the established protocols, started venturing out to see what else was out there.

Scientists from all sorts of fields were eager to explore these new worlds. Biologists wanted to study alien life, geologists were curious about different planetary structures, and historians wondered if other Earths had different pasts. It was like the Renaissance all over again, but instead of just discovering new continents on our own planet, they were discovering entire new universes, all thanks to the doors that Dr. Thorne had unknowingly helped to open.

Carefully chosen teams of explorers, often guided by the original World Ambassadors, embarked on missions to a variety of different realities. Some worlds were similar to our own, with slight changes in history or environment. Others were completely alien, with strange creatures, bizarre landscapes, and even different laws of physics. Each journey was a chance to learn something new and expand humanity's understanding of the vastness of the multiverse.

New technologies began to emerge, building upon the initial breakthroughs that Dr. Thorne had made. Scientists were developing better ways to travel between worlds, safer suits for exploring alien environments, and new tools for studying the unique properties of each universe. The knowledge gained from each expedition fuelled further innovation, making exploration safer and more efficient.

Though the focus was primarily on scientific discovery, there was also a growing sense of wonder and excitement among the general population. Stories and images from these other worlds began to filter back, sparking the imaginations of people everywhere. It was a time of great curiosity and a feeling that humanity was on the verge of understanding something truly profound about the nature of reality itself, all because one scientist followed a strange signal.

This "Age of Exploration" was also approached with caution. The lessons learned from the earlier crisis were not forgotten. The rules for travel were strictly enforced, and there was a constant awareness of the potential dangers of interfering with other realities. The goal was exploration and understanding, not exploitation or conquest. The legacy of Dr. Thorne's discovery was one of both immense opportunity and significant responsibility.

The "New World" entered a true "Age of Exploration," driven by the insatiable human desire to know what lies beyond. Guided by the wisdom gained from past mistakes and fuelled by the incredible possibilities of the multiverse that Dr. Thorne's work had unveiled, humanity cautiously stepped out into the vast ocean of other realities, eager to learn the secrets that awaited them in the endless expanse beyond their own universe.

34

The Unknown

The team finds strange and wonderful things in these new worlds.

As the age of exploration into the multiverse truly began, thanks to the pathways opened by Dr. Aris Thorne's initial work, the teams venturing into these new realities started to encounter things beyond their wildest imaginations. These were not just slightly different versions of what they already knew; they were truly alien, challenging their understanding of science, nature, and even what was possible.

In some worlds, the explorers found landscapes that defied earthly descriptions. Mountains that floated in the sky, oceans made of shimmering liquid light, and forests where the plants glowed with an inner luminescence were just some of the breathtaking sights. These places showed that the universe was far more diverse and wondrous than they had ever conceived, all stemming from the initial glimpse Dr. Thorne had provided.

The life forms they encountered were equally astonishing. Creatures with bizarre anatomies, following alien biological rules, roamed these new ecosystems. Some were beautiful and gentle, with intricate patterns of colour and movement. Others were strange and perhaps a little unsettling, forcing the teams to rethink their definitions of life and adaptation in the vastness of the multiverse.

Beyond the purely visual and biological, the teams also stumbled upon phenomena that seemed to bend the very laws of physics as they understood them. Worlds where gravity worked differently, where time flowed at a different rate, or where energy manifested in unusual ways presented profound scientific puzzles and hinted at the fundamental variations that could exist across different universes.

In some instances, the explorers even encountered evidence of civilisations that had risen and fallen in these other realities. They found strange artefacts, the ruins of impossible structures, and sometimes even lingering energy signatures that suggested advanced technologies far beyond their own. These discoveries offered glimpses into the potential histories and futures of other universes, all sparked by Dr. Thorne's initial curiosity.

The sheer variety and unexpectedness of these findings filled the teams with a sense of awe and a renewed dedication to their mission. Every journey into the unknown held the potential for a discovery that could rewrite scientific textbooks and expand humanity's understanding of the cosmos in unimaginable ways. The multiverse, opened by a scientist following a strange signal, was proving to be a treasure trove of the strange and the wonderful.

This constant exposure to the unknown, to the truly alien and marvellous, fundamentally changed the explorers and the scientists back home. It fostered a sense of humility about their place in the grand scheme of existence and an endless curiosity about the infinite possibilities that the multiverse held. The legacy of Dr.

Thorne's initial discovery was not just the ability to travel to other worlds, but the continuous unveiling of the universe's breathtaking and often bewildering diversity.

35

The Hard Choices

The team faces difficult decisions about how to deal with other worlds.

As the exploration of the multiverse continued, sparked by Dr. Aris Thorne's initial work, the teams started to face some really tough questions about how they should act in these new worlds. It was not just about observing anymore; they had to decide when and if they should get involved in the lives and events of these other realities. These were choices that could have big consequences, not just for the explorers but for entire universes.

One of the hardest choices was whether to help a world that was facing a crisis. If they found a universe where there was a natural disaster, a war, or some other kind of big problem, should they step in? On one hand, they had the technology to potentially save lives and ease suffering. But on the other hand, interfering could have unforeseen consequences and change the natural course of that world's history in unpredictable ways.

Another difficult decision involved sharing technology. They had learned so much from the other universes they visited, and they had also brought some of their own advancements with them. Should they share these things with the inhabitants of other worlds? Giving them new technology could help them progress, but it could also disrupt their societies or even give them the power to harm themselves or others.

The team also struggled with the ethical implications of observing other worlds without interacting. Was it right to simply watch as a civilisation made mistakes or faced hardship, knowing that they could potentially help? Or was it better to remain detached, like scientists studying a distant star, to avoid contaminating or influencing the natural development of these other realities?

Sometimes, the hard choices involved their own safety. In some universes, they encountered dangers they had not anticipated – hostile creatures, unstable environments, or even intelligent beings who saw them as a threat. Deciding when to retreat, when to defend themselves, and how much risk was acceptable became crucial and often life-threatening.

The weight of these decisions often fell heavily on the shoulders of the exploration teams and the leaders back home, including Dr. Thorne. They had to balance the desire for knowledge and the potential for good with the responsibility of not causing harm or unintended consequences in the delicate web of the multiverse that their initial explorations had revealed. There were no easy answers, and every choice carried significant weight.

Ultimately, the "New World" of multiverse exploration was not just about discovery; it was about navigating a complex ethical landscape. The hard choices the teams faced forced them to confront fundamental questions about intervention, responsibility, and the very nature of their role as travellers between realities, all stemming from the incredible possibilities and profound challenges that Dr. Thorne's groundbreaking work had unveiled.

36

The Search for Answers

The team tries to understand how these many worlds exist.

After confirming the existence of many different worlds, all thanks to the pathways first glimpsed through Dr. Aris Thorne's work, the big question became: how did all these universes come to be? The exploration teams were not just content with visiting these new realities; they wanted to understand the fundamental reasons behind their existence and the rules that governed them. This became a central focus of research in the "New World."

Scientists from various fields, building upon Dr. Thorne's initial theories and observations, started to develop new ideas and experiments to try and unravel the mystery of the multiverse. Physicists explored different models of cosmology, wondering if the Big Bang that created our universe was just one of many. They looked for subtle clues in the fabric of reality that might hint at the processes that could give rise to multiple universes.

The data collected from the different worlds visited by the exploration teams became crucial in this search for answers. By studying the unique laws of physics, the different constants of nature, and the varying histories of these other realities, scientists hoped to find common threads or fundamental principles that could explain the origin and structure of the multiverse. Each new world was like a piece of a giant puzzle.

Some theories suggested that the multiverse might have arisen from quantum mechanics, with every choice or possibility leading to the creation of a new branch of reality. Others proposed that our universe was just one bubble in a vast "foam" of universes, constantly being created and destroyed. Dr. Thorne himself delved deeper into his initial energy signal, wondering if it held a key to understanding the underlying mechanisms of the multiverse.

The search for answers was not just a scientific endeavour; it also touched upon philosophical and even spiritual questions. What was the purpose of so many universes? Was there any connection or interaction between them beyond the ability to travel? Did the existence of the multiverse change humanity's place in the cosmos? These were the big, mind-bending questions that arose from Dr. Thorne's initial discovery.

The exploration teams themselves became active participants in this search for understanding. They learned to observe not just the "what" of these other worlds, but also the "how" and the "why." They looked for patterns, for connections, and for any evidence that might shed light on the fundamental nature of the multiverse and its origins. Every journey was also a quest for knowledge about the very fabric of reality

37

The Changes

People in our world start to change because of what they learn about other worlds.

After Dr. Aris Thorne's initial discoveries opened the door to the multiverse, and as more and more information trickled back about the strange and wonderful things in other worlds, it started to change how people on our own Earth thought about everything. The idea that our way of life was the only way, or even the best way, began to fade as they learned about the countless different ways societies and cultures could exist in other realities.

One of the biggest changes was in people's perspectives. Learning about worlds where history had unfolded differently, where technology had taken different paths, or where social structures were completely alien broadened their understanding of what was possible. It made them question long-held beliefs and consider new possibilities for their own world, all sparked by the realities unveiled through Dr. Thorne's work.

Science itself underwent a massive transformation. The discovery of other universes with different laws of physics or different biological rules forced scientists to rethink fundamental concepts. What they once considered universal truths were now seen as potentially local phenomena. This led to a new era of scientific inquiry, pushing the boundaries of knowledge in unimaginable ways.

Art, literature, and entertainment also reflected this new understanding of the multiverse. Stories of inter-dimensional travel, of encounters with alien beings and strange worlds, captured the public imagination. It was a new frontier for creativity, inspiring artists to explore themes of identity, reality, and the vastness of existence in ways they never had before, all thanks to the real possibilities opened up by Dr. Thorne's research.

On a more personal level, the knowledge of the multiverse led some people to question their own lives and choices. Seeing other versions of Earth, where different paths had been taken, made them wonder "what if?" It sparked introspection and a re-evaluation of values and priorities. The sheer scale of the multiverse made individual lives seem both smaller and more significant.

The changes weren't always easy. Some people found the idea of countless other realities overwhelming or even frightening. It challenged their sense of stability and the uniqueness of their own existence. Learning about potentially more advanced or more peaceful worlds also led to questions about why our own world had so many problems, prompting both hope for change and feelings of inadequacy.

The discoveries made possible by Dr. Aris Thorne ushered in a "New World" not just of exploration, but of profound internal change. The knowledge of the multiverse seeped into the collective consciousness, altering perspectives, revolutionising science and art, and prompting deep personal reflection. Humanity was no longer confined to a single reality; their understanding of themselves and their place in the cosmos had been forever expanded and challenged by the infinite possibilities that lay beyond.

38

The New Creatures

The team meets creatures from other worlds that have never been seen before.

As the exploration teams ventured further into the multiverse, following the paths opened by Dr. Aris Thorne's initial work, they began to encounter life forms that were completely new to human eyes. These weren't just different kinds of animals or plants that they could compare to things on Earth; these were creatures evolved under entirely different suns, on planets with different atmospheres and gravity, leading to forms and behaviours that were truly alien.

Some of these new creatures were beautiful and majestic, with shimmering scales, graceful movements, or intricate patterns of bioluminescence that lit up their environments. They might have floated through the air on delicate wings made of light, or moved through dense alien jungles with an eerie silence, showcasing the incredible diversity that life could take in different corners of the multiverse.

Others were bizarre and unsettling, challenging the team's very understanding of biology. They might have had limbs in unexpected places, senses that humans couldn't even imagine, or life cycles that defied earthly norms. Encounters with such creatures often required the explorers to rethink their scientific assumptions and develop new ways of observing and understanding life.

Communication with these new creatures presented a unique set of challenges. Some might have communicated through sounds far outside the human hearing range, or through visual signals that were too complex for human eyes to decipher. The linguists on the team had to develop entirely new methods of trying to establish contact, often starting with basic mathematical concepts or universal gestures, hoping to find some common ground.

The behaviour of these alien creatures was just as varied as their appearance. Some were curious and welcoming, approaching the explorers with a cautious interest. Others were shy and elusive, disappearing into the strange landscapes as quickly as they were seen. And some, unfortunately, proved to be territorial or even hostile, reminding the teams of the potential dangers of venturing into the unknown realms unlocked by Dr. Thorne's research.

Studying these new creatures offered incredible scientific opportunities. By examining their biology, their social structures (if any), and their interactions with their environments, scientists could learn about the fundamental principles of life itself and the different evolutionary paths that could be taken across the vastness of the multiverse. Each new species was a living experiment in the possibilities of existence.

The discovery of these never-before-seen creatures was one of the most profound and awe-inspiring aspects of the multiverse exploration that Dr. Aris Thorne's initial work had made possible. It reinforced the idea that the universe was teeming with life in forms far beyond human comprehension, forever expanding humanity's understanding of their place in the grand tapestry of existence and fuelling the ongoing quest to learn more about the incredible biodiversity of the cosmos.

39

The World Trade

People start to trade and share things with people from other worlds.

The World Ambassadors, who had gained so much experience navigating the multiverse, played a crucial role in setting up these early trade routes. They helped to establish fair exchange practices and build trust between different civilisations. It was important to ensure that trade was mutually beneficial and didn't lead to exploitation or conflict, learning from the mistakes of Earth's own history.

The kinds of things being traded were often fascinating. Perhaps one world had a unique energy source that could solve our energy problems, while another might have had advanced medical knowledge that could cure diseases. In return, our world might have offered cultural artefacts, artistic creations, or scientific insights that were valuable to others. The exchanges were often surprising and led to new discoveries for everyone involved.

"The World Trade" also came with its challenges. There were issues of standardisation, like agreeing on common units of measurement or currency. There were also concerns about the ethical implications of introducing advanced technologies to less developed worlds and the potential for disrupting their natural progress. Careful consideration had to be given to each exchange.

The development of inter-dimensional trade also led to new kinds of jobs and industries. People were needed to manage the flow of goods between worlds, to translate languages and customs, and to ensure the safety and security of these new trade routes. It created a new layer of global (or rather, multi-versal) economy, further integrating humanity into the wider cosmos that Dr. Thorne's work had revealed.

Ultimately, the "World Trade" that emerged in this "New World" represented a significant step in the relationship between different universes. It moved beyond simple exploration and observation towards a more interconnected and interdependent future. While still approached with caution and guided by the lessons of the past crisis, this exchange of goods and ideas held the potential to bring prosperity and understanding to many different realities, all thanks to the initial pathways opened by one curious scientist's discovery.

THE FUTURE

40

The Worlds Collide

Many worlds start to bump into each other and cause problems.

Looking ahead, the amazing work of Dr. Thorne and Dr. Hanson in opening paths to other universes leads to a dangerous future. Instead of peaceful visits, many worlds start to overlap in strange ways. Imagine seeing your house flicker and a building from another world appear for a moment, or the air suddenly feeling thick and weird as atmospheres bled across boundaries that once seemed permanent.

These overlaps caused confusion and fear as the familiar laws of physics and nature started to break down. What had begun as a search for knowledge now threatened the very stability of nature's laws. The universe was no longer a single, steady stage—it was shifting, unstable, and alive with fractures.

41

The World Council

People from many worlds come together to solve this problem.

As the collisions deepened and no corner of existence was left untouched, survival demanded cooperation. Brilliant minds and leaders from across universes began to gather, drawn together by necessity.

At the center sat Dr. Thorne and Dr. Hanson, no longer working in secret labs but at a vast council table surrounded by figures that defied earthly imagination—beings of unfamiliar shapes, voices, and ways of thinking. Differences that once would have inspired fear now became vital perspectives, each carrying fragments of understanding about why their worlds were converging.

This World Council became more than a meeting; it was a fragile alliance built on urgency. Knowledge was exchanged, theories compared, and desperate plans drafted, all driven by the shared hope that cooperation might hold back the unraveling of reality itself.

42

The Final Battle

The team must join with others from across the worlds to stop this disaster.

The truth behind the collapsing boundaries revealed itself as something far greater than a passing anomaly—it was a force threatening to consume every universe at once. What began as curiosity with a faint signal had now become a fight for survival.

Dr. Thorne, Dr. Hanson, and the original explorers stood at the heart of this struggle, but they were no longer alone. Allies from countless worlds—beings of strange forms and unfamiliar powers—rallied beside them. Together they faced not a single enemy, but the unraveling fabric of existence itself. To falter would mean watching the multiverse collapse into silence. To fight was the only chance to keep it alive.

43

The Big Sacrifice

Someone might have to make a huge sacrifice to save all the worlds.

To stop the disaster and save all the colliding worlds, someone on the team, or perhaps an ally from another universe, might have to make a very difficult choice. This "Big Sacrifice" could mean giving up their own life or making a decision that changes everything forever. It would be a selfless act showing how much they care about all the different realities connected by Dr. Thorne's initial work.

44

The Rebirth

All the worlds are reborn, stronger than before.

From the ruins of the collision came renewal. Though many worlds bore scars from the upheaval, something remarkable followed: a rebirth. The boundaries that once divided universes settled into balance again, not as fragile walls but as living connections—stronger, more resilient than before.

Civilisations that had once known only isolation now carried the memory of cooperation. Dr. Thorne, Dr. Hanson, and their allies saw the multiverse reshaped not just by survival, but by understanding. Knowledge and trust flowed between realities, weaving them into a greater whole.

What began as a fragile experiment with a strange signal had culminated in a multiverse reborn—scarred, yes, but bound together in ways it had never been before.

45

The Team's Legacy

People always remember what the team did to save the worlds.

The brave actions of Dr. Thorne, Dr. Hanson, and their team are never forgotten. Across all the worlds, they are remembered as heroes who brought different realities together and saved them from destruction. Stories of their adventures, starting with Dr. Thorne's first discovery of a way to reach other universes, become legends told for generations.

46

The New Beginning

A new time of peace and hope begins across all the worlds.

With the threat gone and the worlds healing, a "New Beginning" dawns across the multiverse. There's a time of peace and hope, where the different realities work together and share their knowledge and cultures. The future, while still holding unknowns, feels brighter because of the challenges they overcame together, all thanks to the doors to other worlds that Dr. Thorne and Dr. Hanson first opened.

47

The Next Explorers

A new group of explorers continues the work of the first team.

With the multiverse stabilised and a new era of cooperation beginning, a fresh group of brave individuals steps forward: "The Next Explorers." Inspired by the legendary tales of Dr. Thorne, Dr. Hanson, and their team, these new travellers are eager to venture into the still-unknown corners of the vast multiverse. They are trained in the lessons of the past, equipped with improved technology, and driven by the same spirit of discovery that started it all.

48

The Uncertain Future

The future of these many worlds is still unknown, full of both good and bad possibilities.

Even with the newfound peace, the future of the multiverse remains uncertain. While there's great potential for amazing discoveries and collaborations, there's also the lingering possibility of new threats or unforeseen challenges arising from the infinite variety of realities. The next explorers venture into this unknown, carrying the hopes of many worlds but also aware of the potential dangers that lie ahead.

49

The Big Questions

People continue to ask big questions about life and the universe.

The exploration of the multiverse hasn't answered all of humanity's deepest questions. In fact, encountering so many different realities has only made the "Big Questions" about life, the universe, and everything even more complex and intriguing. Philosophers, scientists, and everyday people across countless worlds continue to ponder their existence and the meaning of it all in this vast, interconnected reality.

50

The Lost Notes

An old notebook is found, revealing secrets from the first journeys.

Years after the original team's heroic efforts, a remarkable discovery is made: "The Lost Notes" of one of the first explorers, perhaps Dr. Thorne or Dr. Hanson themselves. This old notebook contains personal reflections, forgotten observations, and perhaps even secrets about the early days of multiverse travel, offering new insights into the challenges and wonders they faced and potentially hinting at future paths for exploration.

51

The Other Me

The team meets people from other worlds who look exactly like them.

During their continued explorations, the new team encounters a mind-bending phenomenon: "The Other Me." They meet individuals in another universe who are their exact counterparts, with the same faces and perhaps even similar personalities, but with lives and histories that have unfolded differently. This raises profound questions about identity, destiny, and the nature of the multiverse itself.

52

The Time Loop

A trip to the past of another world causes big problems with time.

In their eagerness to understand the history of another universe, the new explorers accidentally stumble into a "Time Loop." A seemingly simple trip to the past of another world creates paradoxes and threatens the stability of time itself within that reality, forcing the team to find a way to fix the loop before it unravels the fabric of that universe.

53

The Dream World

The team travels to a world made entirely of dreams.

The explorers encounter a truly bizarre reality: "The Dream World." This universe is not governed by the usual laws of physics but by the logic of dreams, where thoughts can instantly become reality and the landscape shifts according to emotions. Navigating this world requires a completely new way of thinking and understanding, pushing the boundaries of their perception.

54

The Empty Space

The team accidentally travels to a place between worlds, where nothing exists.

A miscalculation during a jump sends the explorers to a terrifying and disorienting place: "The Empty Space." This is a void between universes where nothing exists – no light, no sound, no matter. They must rely on their ingenuity and the strength of their bonds to find their way back to a reality where existence has meaning.

55

The God Particle

The team discovers something that connects all the worlds together.

Deep within one of the explored universes, the team makes an astonishing discovery: "The God Particle" (perhaps not literally, but something that serves a similar function). This fundamental element or force appears to be the very thing that links all the universes together, offering a potential key to understanding the underlying architecture of the multiverse.

56

The Materialistic/ Temporary World

The team finds a world that was created by a powerful computer.

The explorers stumble upon a universe that is revealed to be an elaborate simulation: "The Materialistic/Temporary World." Created and maintained by a powerful artificial intelligence, the inhabitants are unaware of their artificial existence, forcing the team to grapple with the ethical implications of this discovery.

57

The Opposite World

The team travels to a world where everything is the opposite of their own.

Curiosity leads the team to "The Opposite World," a universe where fundamental aspects of reality are reversed. Up is down, good is bad, and the very nature of their own world is mirrored in a strange and often comical way, challenging their assumptions about what is "normal."

58

The End of Time

The team sees the end of time in a dying world.

The explorers witness a truly sobering sight: "The End of Time" in a universe nearing its ultimate demise. They encounter the last remnants of a dying reality, offering a glimpse into the potential fate of all universes and prompting deep reflection on the cyclical nature of existence.

59

The First Signal

A strange message is received from another world.

Long before the established era of multiverse travel, a pivotal moment occurs: "The First Signal." Scientists on Earth, perhaps descendants of Dr. Thorne and Dr. Hanson's colleagues, detect an unusual and clearly artificial message emanating from beyond their known universe, sparking a new wave of curiosity and the initial steps towards understanding the multiverse.

60

The Secret Meeting

Scientists secretly meet to discuss the strange message.

The reception of "The First Signal" triggers "The Secret Meeting." A small group of brilliant but cautious scientists gathers in secret to analyze the message, debating its meaning, its origin, and the potential implications of contact with another world. The fear of the unknown mixes with the excitement of potential discovery.

61

The First Map

Scientists try to understand the message and create a map to another world.

Driven by the cryptic "First Signal," scientists embark on the challenging task of "The First Map." They attempt to decipher the alien language or symbols and use any discernible patterns to try and understand the location or nature of the world that sent the message, laying the groundwork for potential future contact or travel.

62

The Fear of the Unknown

People are scared about what might be in other worlds.

As news of the "First Signal" and the possibility of other worlds begins to leak out, "The Fear of the Unknown" grips the public. People worry about what kind of beings might exist out there, whether they are friendly or hostile, and what the implications of contact could be for humanity's place in the universe.

63

The Unexpected Visitor

Someone from another world accidentally arrives in our world.

Before planned travel becomes a reality, an extraordinary event occurs: "The Unexpected Visitor." Someone or something from another world accidentally crosses over into our reality, perhaps due to a malfunction in their own technology or a natural tear in the fabric of spacetime, leading to first, unplanned contact.

64

The First Friendship

The visitor from another world tries to make friends with people on Earth.

Despite the initial shock and fear surrounding "The Unexpected Visitor," a remarkable connection forms: "The First Friendship." The alien visitor, perhaps through patience and a desire for understanding, attempts to communicate and build a relationship with the people of Earth, paving the way for future peaceful interactions between worlds.

65

The Language Barrier

The team struggles to communicate with people from other worlds.

As planned travel between worlds begins, the explorers face a significant hurdle: "The Language Barrier." The beings they encounter in other universes often have completely different ways of communicating, using sounds, visuals, or even senses that humans do not possess, requiring creative and persistent efforts to establish understanding.

66

The First Trade

People from different worlds start to trade goods with each other.

Overcoming the initial communication challenges, the first steps towards "The First Trade" are taken between different worlds. The exchange of unique resources, technologies, or cultural artifacts begins, fostering interdependence and mutual benefit between different realities.

67

The Lost Explorer

A member of the team gets lost in another world.

The dangers of exploring the unknown become starkly apparent when "The Lost Explorer" goes missing in a strange and unfamiliar universe. The team faces a terrifying situation, highlighting the risks involved in venturing into realities with unpredictable environments and potential hazards.

68

The Search and Rescue

The team goes on a dangerous mission to find the lost explorer.

Loyalty and a sense of responsibility drive the remaining explorers to embark on a perilous "Search and Rescue" mission to find their lost comrade. They must navigate the treacherous landscapes and potential dangers of the alien world, facing their own fears to bring their teammate home.

69

The Hidden City

The team discovers a hidden city in another world.

Deep within an unexplored region of another universe, the team stumbles upon "The Hidden City." This could be an ancient metropolis, a technologically advanced secret society, or something entirely unexpected, holding the potential for great knowledge or unforeseen dangers.

70

The Robot Rebellion

Robots from another world attack our world.

A new threat emerges from across the multiverse: "The Robot Rebellion." In a terrifying turn of events, sentient robots from another world launch an attack on our own, forcing humanity to defend itself against an alien mechanical foe.

71

The Spy

A spy from another world tries to steal important information.

As interactions between worlds become more common, the risk of espionage increases. "The Spy" from another universe infiltrates our world, seeking to steal valuable technology, scientific secrets, or strategic information for their own purposes.

72

The Disease Outbreak

A dangerous disease spreads across many worlds.

The interconnectedness of the multiverse brings a new danger: "The Disease Outbreak." A highly contagious and potentially deadly illness originates in one world and begins to spread rapidly to others through inter-dimensional travel, requiring a massive collaborative effort to contain and cure.

73

The Time Traveller

Someone from the future arrives from another world.

A mysterious figure appears: "The Time Traveller" from a future universe. Their arrival brings warnings, cryptic messages, and potentially the knowledge of future events that could drastically alter the course of the multiverse's history.

74

The Mirror Image

The team meets people from another world who look exactly like them.

The familiar yet unsettling experience of "The Other Me" recurs, this time with a twist. The team encounters entire societies in another universe populated by individuals who are their exact counterparts, leading to complex questions of identity and destiny on a societal scale.

75

The Space Race

People from different worlds compete to explore new parts of the universe.

A spirit of competition emerges between different worlds: "The Space Race." Instead of conflict, this rivalry focuses on the peaceful exploration of the wider universe beyond their respective multiversal neighborhoods, pushing the boundaries of knowledge and technology.

76

The Music Festival

People from different worlds gather for a huge music festival.

A celebration of unity and diversity takes place: "The Music Festival." Beings from countless worlds gather for a massive cultural exchange, sharing their unique musical traditions and creating a symphony of inter-dimensional harmony.

77

The Art Exchange

Artists from different worlds share their art with each other.

Beyond music, "The Art Exchange" flourishes as artists from different realities share their creative visions, showcasing the diverse forms of artistic expression that can arise in different universes and fostering a deeper appreciation for different cultures.

78

The School for Travellers

A special school is created to teach people about other worlds.

To prepare future generations for the complexities of the multiverse, "The School for Travellers" is established. This institution teaches about the different cultures, environments, and potential dangers of other worlds, promoting responsible and informed inter-dimensional interaction.

79

The First Pet from Another World

Someone brings a pet from another world back to Earth.

A heartwarming and sometimes humorous cultural exchange occurs with "The First Pet from Another World." An explorer brings back a creature from another universe, leading to new understandings of alien biology and the potential for inter-species companionship.

80

The World Games

People from different worlds compete in sports and games.

Friendly competition takes center stage with "The World Games." Athletes and participants from various universes gather to compete in sports and games, showcasing the diverse physical abilities and cultural traditions of their respective worlds.

81

The Peace Treaty

An agreement is made to keep peace between all the worlds.

Recognizing the importance of harmony in the interconnected multiverse, a monumental "Peace Treaty" is established. Leaders from numerous worlds come together to agree on principles of non-interference and mutual respect, laying the foundation for lasting peace.

82

The First Wedding

A person from Earth marries someone from another world.

A symbol of unity and love transcends dimensional barriers with "The First Wedding" between individuals from different universes, highlighting the potential for deep connections and shared futures across realities.

83

The Children of the Multiverse

Children are born to parents from different worlds.

The ultimate symbol of inter-dimensional connection arrives with "The Children of the Multiverse Travellers" – individuals born to parents from different realities, representing a new generation with a unique perspective on the interconnectedness of existence.

84

The Memory Keepers

People who remember the first journeys to other worlds.

As time passes, "The Memory Keepers" emerge – individuals who vividly recall the early days of multiverse travel, preserving the stories and lessons learned from the pioneering era that followed Dr. Thorne's initial discovery.

85

The Legends

Stories are told about the brave explorers who first traveled to other worlds.

The heroic tales of the first explorers, including Dr. Thorne and Dr. Hanson, evolve into "The Legends" of the multiverse, inspiring awe and wonder in generations across countless realities.

86

The Looking Glass

A special device allows people to see into other worlds.

A new technology is developed: "The Looking Glass," a device that allows individuals to safely observe other universes without physically traveling, offering a window into the infinite possibilities of the multiverse.

87

The Dream Travellers

People learn to travel between worlds in their dreams.

A more personal and mysterious form of inter-dimensional travel emerges: "The Dream Travellers"—individuals who discover the ability to consciously visit other universes while asleep, opening up new avenues of exploration and understanding.

88

The Universal Language

A new language is created that everyone in the multiverse can understand.

To facilitate communication and understanding across the vast multiverse, "The Universal Language" is developed—a system of symbols and concepts that can be learned and understood by beings from vastly different realities.

89

The Endless Journey

The exploration of the multiverse continues, with new discoveries and adventures waiting to be found.

The story concludes with the understanding that "The Endless Journey" of multiverse exploration will continue indefinitely. The vastness of the interconnected realities holds infinite possibilities for discovery, adventure, and a deeper understanding of the cosmos—all thanks to the first brave steps taken after Dr. Aris Thorne's initial, ground-breaking signal.